HARRY THE ELEPHANT HAS AN ALLERGY

Written By: KERRI LOUISE

Illustrated by: Jimmy Carroll

ISBN: 9781700354167

FOR CAMERON, HARRISON, AND TOMMY 2

You inspire me everyday to be a better person. Without you even knowing it, you've taught me to look beyond my weaknesses, change my mindset and prevail. My unconditional love for you has given me more super powers than I could ever imagine. Because of you, I feel like there's nothing I can't do. I hope as you journey through life that you find your super powers too. Please know that no single person, no allergy, no bumps in the road could ever take away your power to be the best you.
You'll never be sitting at the peanut free table alone, because I'm here for you always.
LOVE, MOM

ACKNOWLEDGMENTS

Thanks to the North Rockland school district for not only being one of the best school systems that my children attend, but for allowing me to come into your schools to practice reading this book. A Special thanks to the teachers who never let Harry feel alone at the peanut free table. Much appreciation to Jen Kittner, Kristy Ellis, Nancy Donahue, Sharon Mulrean, Kirsten Laier, for their thoughts, advice and for welcoming me into their classrooms.

Thank you Kelly Haglund for being one of my oldest and smartest friends. Thanks for all your wonderful wisdom, editing, guidance and motivation. Knowing you would never let me sit at the peanut free table alone, is knowing that I have one of the best friends for life.

This book came alive the very day I chatted with the extremely, funny comedian and illustrator of this book Jimmy Carroll. Cheers to you for being so easy to work with and for your expertise. You drew an awesome peanut free table and you turned my dreams into animated, funny, little characters that makes this book outstanding.
Your talents are without measure and I encourage everyone to check out his children's book
Called "Now my name is Moose."

Thank you to my husband and comedian Tom Cotter. Without you I'm nothing and our beautiful children would not exist. You are the best husband and father in the world and one of the funniest men alive without question.
Go see for yourself at: www.tomcotter.com
Not only would you join us at the peanut free table, you would make us all laugh the whole time too!

Harry was right in the middle of doing a handstand at his circus school, when all of a sudden,

"Aha Aha Ahhh Chooooooo!!"

Harry sneezed and rolled all the way out of the circus tent, down the hill and landed in his front yard. He dusted himself off, walked all the way back up the hill and the second he got back into the tent, "Ahhhh Ahhhh Ahhh Choo!!" Harry sneezed again!

This time his sneeze was so hard he rolled all the way down the hill, across his front yard and got stuck in his front door. All you could see was Harry's big elephant rump stuck right in the door of his home.

Harry cried out, "Mommy I'm stuck! I'm stuck! I can't get out!"

And before Harry's mommy could do anything,

"Aha Aha Ahhh Choooooo!!"

he sneezed again and that got him out of the doorway, onto the patio, hitting the picnic table, knocking off the flower pot, which flew high up into the air and landed right on top of Harry's head.

"My baby is sick!" said Harry's mom. "I'm taking you to the doctor."

The doctor did some special tests and found out that Harry was sneezing so much because… he was allergic to peanuts!

 It's true! Even the Doctor couldn't believe it! That's all elephants do all day- is eat peanuts!

His mother couldn't believe it. That's all she does all day is eat peanuts. How could her son be allergic to peanuts? But he was.

The next day his mom had to go to the Elephant Circus School and tell all his teachers that Harry couldn't eat peanuts. She gave the school nurse special medicine just in case he got sick by accidentally eating peanuts.
And he had to eat at the "peanut free" table at lunch.

Harry was all alone because no one else was allergic to peanuts.

He was so sad he couldn't possibly practice his handstand with the rest of the kids at school, so he went into the circus garden to see the flowers.

Just then Buzzy The Bee came along and landed right on his nose and said, "Hey Harry, why such the long trunk?" "I'm allergic to peanuts," said Harry.

 Said Buzzy The Bee. "You've got to be kidding me! Well, cheer up, because you're not alone. Guess what I'm allergic to? Honey!" Whispered the bee. "Honey?" asked Harry in disbelief."

"Yes, honey," said the bee. I can't go near the stuff, it makes my stripes itchy."

"Well, only the yellow stripes, the black ones stay the same, but OHHH do those yellow stripes get itchy."

"But that's all bees do, all day, is make honey," said Harry. "That's right!" said Buzzy.

"Then what do you do?" Harry asked. "Well, I've made the best of it. Since I can't go near honey, my job is to protect the hive. I'm real good at it too. I won a trophy for being the best beehive protector."

Buzzy did a loop-de-loop around harry's head and continued, "Come meet some of my friends. This is Cam The Cow, she's allergic to milk." "You're allergic to milk?" laughed Harry.

"I know what you're going to say, that's all cows do, all day, is make milk. Well I don't! I can't! I break out in a red, bumpy rash all over my body."

Well not all over my body, only the white spots get the rash. The black spots stay the same."

"Wow," said Harry. "So what do you do all day if you can't make milk?"

"I'm in charge of all the cows. I make sure they get enough food and water so they can make the best milk. You can't make milk without eating right, and I'm good at being in charge. Our wheat farmer won a trophy for having the best tasting milk in town. Did you know our farmer is "Gluten Free" He can't eat anything with wheat in it, but that doesn't stop him from growing wheat and making a living." Explained Cam.

Hmm thought Harry, "I guess I could be good at something too."

"You sure can," said the bee. "Just because you can't do something doesn't mean you can't be great at something else."

"Take a look at my friend Catherine The Chicken. She's allergic to eggs."

"A chicken allergic to eggs you ask? It's true!" shouted Buzzy The Bee.

"But that can't be right," Harry said. "That's all chickens do, all day, is lay eggs."

"Tell me about it!" clucked Catherine, as she ran right out of the henhouse. "I can lay my eggs, but then I've got to get out of there as quick as I can before my eyes start to get all watery."

Well, not both eyes just my right eye, my left eye stays the same.

"You mean to tell me that all you do, all day, is lay eggs and run away from them?" asked Harry.

"As far as I can," said Catherine. "That way I won't feel sick."

"Then why even bother to lay the eggs?" asked Harry.

"Because I'm the best at it! I have the biggest eggs in town," bragged the Catherine The Chicken.

"Let me guess?" said Harry. "You won a trophy for the biggest egg?"

"How did you know that? Did a little birdie tell you that? Tommy 2 Bird maybe?"

"Who is Tommy 2 Bird, and why do you call him Tommy 2 Bird?" asked Harry.

"Because he likes to do two things at the same time. He once knocked off two worms with one stone, and he can't even eat worms because he's allergic to them!"

Harry was shocked, "A bird allergic to worms?"

"Oh yeah," said Catherine. "I didn't believe it myself, I mean, that's all birds do, all day, is eat worms."

"Well, I would love to meet that Tommy 2 Bird," said Harry, "and I'm sure he has a trophy in his nest for something he's done, but it's getting late and I must be going, because tomorrow is the handstand contest at circus school and you know what?"

"I'm going to win that trophy! Just because I can't eat peanuts doesn't mean I can't be the best at handstands!"

Harry ran home as fast as he could. He ate honey and eggs for dinner, as fast as he could. He drank the best milk in town, as fast as he could.

He was so focused on winning that trophy that he skipped dessert – worms dipped in chocolate!

All Harry wanted to do was practice his handstands.

He practiced before and after his homework.

Then he got into his lucky elephant pajamas and he practiced again.

He brushed his teeth and practiced one last time.

The next day at circus school was the big contest.

And guess what?

Harry won!

Harry got a trophy for being the only elephant that could do a handstand on one hand!

Harry put his trophy in the center of his "peanut free" table and he started to eat his lunch all by himself.

Everyone was so happy for Harry and wanted to talk to him about his trophy.

So, one by one, all the elephants put their peanuts to the side, washed their hands, and joined Harry at the "peanut free" table.

They ate eggs, honey, the best milk in town, and worms dipped in chocolate.

As Harry stood up to thank all of his elephant friends, he wished his new found friends could join him.

Then all of a sudden, in the corner of his eye, sitting in the lunch room,

he saw Buzzy The Bee, Cam The Cow, Catherine The Chicken, and Tommy 2 Bird, all smiling with pride for Harry…and

EATING PEANUTS!

THE END

About the author:

Kerri Louise is an elementary school teacher, stand up comedian, actor and author. Her first book is called "Mean Mommy" Tales of motherhood survival from the comedy trenches and was on the top 10 parenting books on Amazon. Kerri Louise has appeared on *Showtime, Oprah, Dr. Oz*, and *Howard Stern*. Kerri was a finalist on NBC's *Last Comic Standing* and starred in her own TV show called *Two Funny*, on The WE Network. These credits plus her very popular Webisode on Youtube called "My Mommy Minute" has made Kerri an attraction at comedy clubs and festivals across the country. She lives in New York with comedian husband, Tom Cotter, and their three sons -Harry, Cam, & Tommy2. Kerri was inspired to write this book because of her son Harry's allergy to nuts and eggs. She hopes It helps all children with allergies not feel alone or limited in their ability to do anything in this world.
She hopes this book makes them laugh and empowers them.
Buy "Mean Mommy" on Amazon now and check out "My Mommy Minute"at:
KerriLouise.com

About the illustrator:

Jimmy Carroll is an Author, Illustrator and Professional Stand-Up Comedian. He has been touring the world as a comedian for the past 35 years. His Stand-up has led him to be seen on Comedy Central, A&E, ESPN II, PBS and he has performed for our Troops Overseas.
When not touring with his comedy show, Jimmy is always writing, Illustrating or creating something. Check out more of Jimmy's work at:
JimmyCarroll.net
TheLastOfTheBoomers.com
ModernManComics.com

Made in the USA
Middletown, DE
12 August 2022